For Evan and George with love – M. R.

With love to Barbara and David – N. E.

PUFFIN BOOKS
Published by the Penguin Group: London, New York,
Australia, Canada, India, Ireland, New Zealand and South Africa
Penguin Books Ltd, Registered Offices: 80 Strand, London WC2R 0RL, England
puffinbooks.com
First published 2013
008
Text copyright © Michelle Robinson, 2013
Illustrations copyright © Nick East, 2013
Made and printed in China
ISBN: 978–0–141–34285–6

Goodnight Tractor

Michelle Robinson

Illustrated by **Nick East**

PUFFIN

The stars are out.
It's time for bed.
So say 'goodnight',
my sleepyhead.

Goodnight farmer.
Goodnight plough.

Goodnight trailer.

Goodnight cow.

Goodnight dog,

and goodnight sheep . . .

Goodnight tractor, time to sleep.

Goodnight combine.

Goodnight truck.

Goodnight
donkey.

Goodnight duck.

Goodnight pig,
	and goodnight sheep . . .

Goodnight tractor, time to sleep.

Goodnight wagon.
Goodnight puddles.

Goodnight horse
and hens in huddles.

Dog and donkey, duck and cow.

Combine, wagon, truck and plough.

Oinks

and brays

and moos

and baas.

Quacks
and
neighs,
and moon and stars.

Goodnight all,

now count the sheep . . .

Goodnight tractor, time to sleep.